For Spencer Banko, who is also wild and funny,
and the best brother ever
—L.M.S.

To Rowan and Elodie
—J.M.

Text copyright © 2012 by Lola M. Schaefer
Illustrations copyright © 2012 by Jessica Meserve
All rights reserved. Published by Disney • Hyperion, an imprint of Disney Book Group.
No part of this book may be reproduced or transmitted in any form or by any means, electronic
or mechanical, including photocopying, recording, or by any information storage
and retrieval system, without written permission from the publisher.
For information address Disney • Hyperion, 125 West End Avenue, New York, New York 10023.
First Edition, March 2012
5 7 9 10 8 6 4
FAC-029191-16239
Printed in Malaysia
Library of Congress Cataloging-in-Publication Data
Schaefer, Lola M., 1950–
One special day / by Lola Schaefer ; illustrated by Jessica Meserve.
—1st ed.   p. cm.
Summary: An energetic and imaginative boy becomes a big brother.
ISBN-13: 978-1-4231-3760-3 • ISBN-10: 1-4231-3760-4
[1. Behavior—Fiction. 2. Brothers—Fiction. 3. Babies–Fiction.] I. Meserve, Jessica, ill. II. Title.
PZ7.S33233On 2012 • [E]—dc23   2011015977
The art was created in digital oil pastel. The type was set in 40-point Chaloops. Designed by Joann Hill.
Reinforced binding
Visit www.DisneyBooks.com

One Special Day

WRITTEN BY
Lola M. Schaefer

ILLUSTRATED BY
Jessica Meserve

Disney • HYPERION

LOS ANGELES   NEW YORK

Spencer was a boy.

He was strong—

strong as a

He was fast—

fast as a

He was tall—

tall as a

He was
LOUD—

He was
funny—

funny as a

He was wild—

He was messy—

messy as a

He was free—

free as a

Until one
special day,

when Spencer
was quiet
and waiting.

And then
he was gentle,

because,
for the first
time ever—

Spencer was a brother.

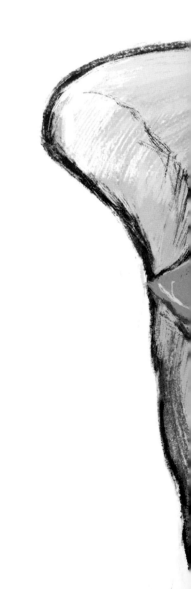